Richard Scarry's
A Day at the Police Station

First published in the USA by Random House in 2004
This edition first published in the UK by HarperCollins *Children's Books* in 2014
Copyright © 2004 by the Richard Scarry Corporation

1 3 5 7 9 10 8 6 4 2

ISBN: 978-0-00-757494-0

www.harpercollins.co.uk

Printed and bound in China

Richard Scarry's
A Day at the
Police Station

It is Friday evening.
The Murphy family has finished
dinner. Mrs Murphy clears the table
while Sergeant Murphy washes
the dishes.

"It's time to get into your
pyjamas and go off to bed,"
Mrs Murphy tells Bridget.

"Run along up to your room and I'll read
you a story!" calls Sergeant Murphy.

While Bridget climbs the stairs, she can hear her parents talking in the kitchen.

"I have to go to Workville tomorrow, Sarge," says Mrs Murphy. "Could you please look after Bridget?"

"Hmmm," replies Sergeant Murphy. "Officer Flo is sick. I have to be on duty for her tomorrow – but I'll just take Bridget to the police station with me. I don't think she'll mind."

But when Sergeant Murphy goes up to Bridget's room, he finds her crying.

"What's the matter, Bridget?" Sergeant Murphy asks.

"I wanted to go to the park tomorrow," Bridget cries. "And now you have to work! I don't like you being a police officer. You're ALWAYS on duty!"

"But being a police officer is very important," says Sergeant Murphy, hugging Bridget. "I'm sorry we can't go to the park, but we'll have a good time at the police station. THAT I can promise!"

The next morning,
Sergeant Murphy and Bridget
ride off to the police station.
"Goodbye, Bridget!" calls
Mrs Murphy. "Goodbye, Sarge!"

On the way, they
come to a junction.
There is a huge traffic jam!
The traffic lights
are broken.

Sergeant Murphy
directs the cars
until Mr Fixit
can come and
repair the lights.

"This is what Daddy calls
a good time?" Bridget says, sulking.
"Watching traffic?"

Just then, Mr Raccoon
comes out of his coffee shop,
bringing Bridget a glass
of milk and a doughnut.

"Your father does a great job, Bridget!" he says. "I don't
know what Busytown would do without him."

Soon Sergeant Murphy and Bridget are on their way again. When they arrive at the police station, the telephone is ringing.

Sergeant Murphy answers it. "Busytown police station. Sergeant Murphy here."

It's Hilda Hippo on the line.

"Oh, Sergeant Murphy, I'm so frightened!
There's a ghost in my bathroom!"
"A GHOST?" Sergeant Murphy replies.
"Just stay calm, Hilda. I'll be right over!"

Sergeant Murphy
and Bridget race over to Hilda's.

When they arrive, Hilda looks as pale as a ghost herself.

"Sergeant Murphy, I haven't slept a wink!" Hilda says nervously. "The ghost has been flushing the toilet all night!"

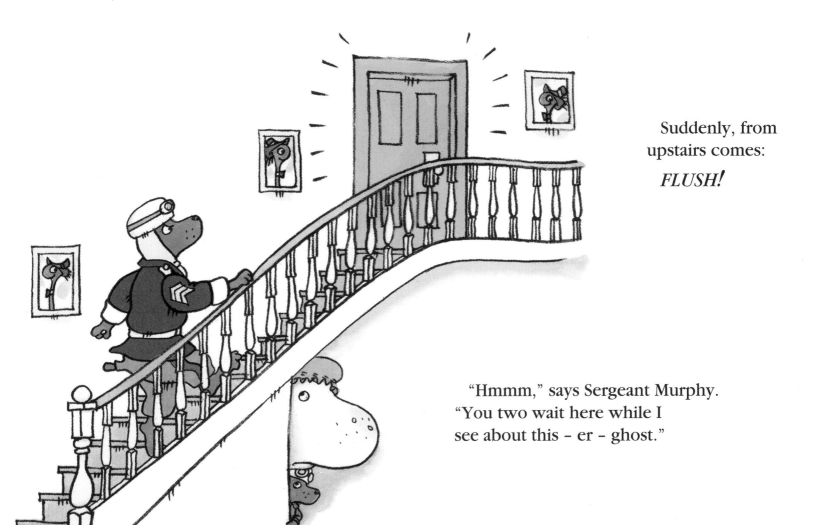

Suddenly, from upstairs comes:

FLUSH!

"Hmmm," says Sergeant Murphy. "You two wait here while I see about this – er – ghost."

He peeks inside,
but the bathroom
is empty.

FLUSH!

goes the toilet again.
Sergeant Murphy
climbs onto the toilet
seat and checks inside
the tank.

"There!" he says.

"The toilet just needed som
adjusting. You shouldn't let y
imagination run away with yo
like that, Hilda!"

On the way back to the police station, they
see a toddler crying in the street.

Sergeant Murphy takes her to the police station.

The phone is ringing when they
arrive. It's the child's mother!
Thank goodness her darling is safe
with Sergeant Murphy. Bridget
plays with the toddler until
her mother comes to fetch her.

Just then, Mr Frumble arrives at the door.
"Excuse me, but has anyone seen my hat?"
he asks. "It's the third one I've lost in
three days!"

Sergeant Murphy makes a note of the lost hat
and promises to call Mr Frumble if it's found.

Minutes after Mr Frumble
leaves, Mr Gronkle storms in.

"I'm here to report a robbery!" he shouts.

"Wow! A real robbery!"
thinks Bridget.

"My car keys have been
stolen," says Mr Gronkle,
"and I know who took
them: Wolfgang Wolf,
Harry Hyena and Benny
Baboon!"

Through the door come Wolfgang, Harry and Benny – each wearing a green hat.

"Did somebody call us?" asks Wolfgang.

"We found these hats," says Harry.

"And we're bringing them here to be returned to their rightful owner!" adds Benny.

"I saw you thieves walking around my car," shouts Mr Gronkle. "You must have stolen my keys! I can't find them anywhere!"

"Now, just a moment, Mr Gronkle!" Sergeant Murphy says. "You have to have some proof before you can accuse someone of stealing."

"We didn't take your keys!" says Wolfgang.

"We'd never steal anything!" says Harry.

"Honest!" adds Benny.

Sergeant Murphy decides they should all go together to the scene of the crime.

"Are THESE your stolen keys?"
Bridget asks Mr Gronkle,
holding up a ring of keys.

"Why, yes!" replies
Mr Gronkle, surprised.
"Wherever did you
find them?"

"Under your car, by the door," says Bridget.

"I guess your 'thief' must have accidental[ly]
dropped them," Sergeant Murphy tells
Mr Gronkle.

"I owe you an apology," Mr Gronkle
says to Wolfgang, Harry and Benny.
"To make up for my mistake, I want to
take you out for ice creams."

As they walk back to the police station, Sergeant Murphy and Bridget see two boys fighting.

Sergeant Murphy runs up and pulls them apart. "Stop that!" he says. "What's this all about?"

"Jimmy won't let me ride his bike!" says Johnny.
"It's MY bike!" shouts Jimmy.

"You need to settle your problems peacefully," Sergeant Murphy tells the boys.

Just then, Bridget hears someone crying, "HELP!"

Sergeant Murphy races
to the edge of the pier.
Bravely, he dives into
the river!

Sergeant Murphy carries
Bananas Gorilla safely out of
the river.
My, isn't he strong!

Then he dives back into the river!
Does he want to go for a swim?

No! He wants to get
Bananas's Bananamobile!
"Please do be careful
when driving near the water,"
Sergeant Murphy tells
Bananas.

Back at the police station,
Sergeant Murphy puts on a
dry uniform.
"We have to hurry, or we'll
be late for school!" he says.

Bridget is confused.
"School? On Saturday?" she wonders.

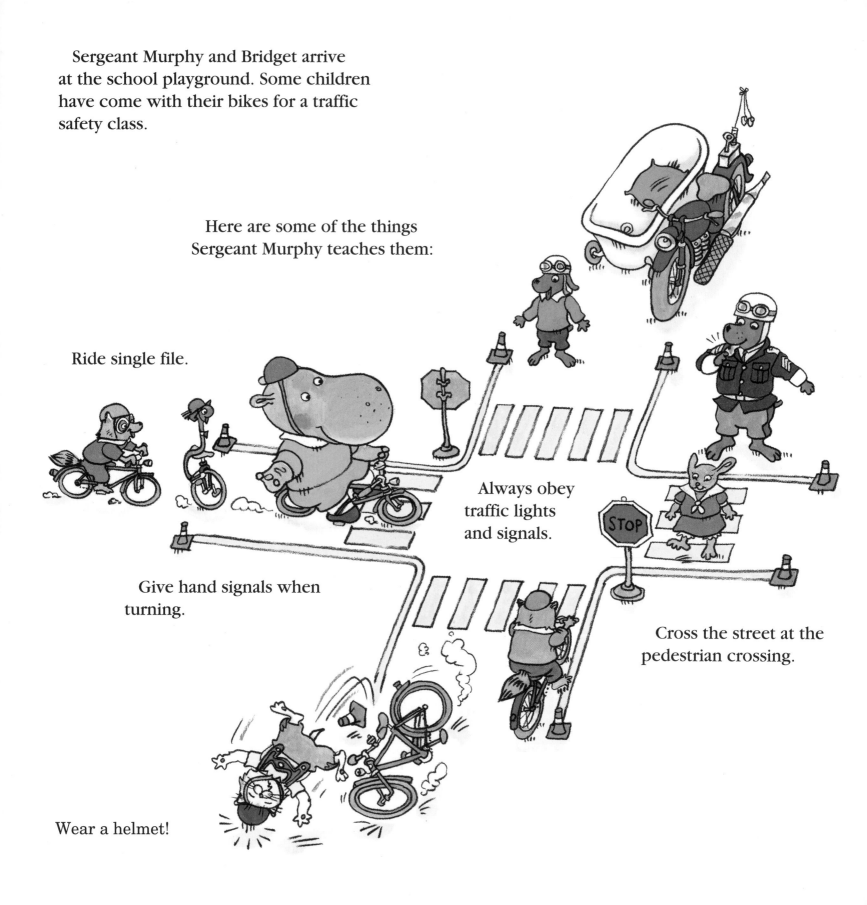

Sergeant Murphy and Bridget arrive at the school playground. Some children have come with their bikes for a traffic safety class.

Here are some of the things Sergeant Murphy teaches them:

Ride single file.

Always obey traffic lights and signals.

Give hand signals when turning.

Cross the street at the pedestrian crossing.

STOP

Wear a helmet!

Make sure your brakes, lights and bell work properly.

And please don't leave
your bike lying around.

Park it properly. Thank you!

"We missed you at the park today, Bridget," Huckle says.
"I was on duty with Daddy all day!" Bridget replies. "We got rid of
a ghost and helped a little girl find her mummy. Then we solved a
robbery, and Daddy stopped two boys who were fighting. Then he
bravely saved Bananas Gorilla from drowning!"

"Wow!" says Huckle. "Having a dad
who's a police officer must be really cool!"

"You bet it is!" replies Bridget.
"I think my daddy has the very
best job EVER!"

"Um – excuse me,
Sergeant Murphy,
but has anyone seen
my hat yet?"

The wonderful world of
Richard Scarry

Enjoy these fantastic Richard Scarry books!

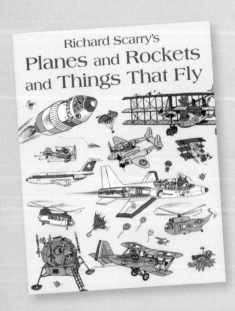

Richard Scarry's Best Lowly Worm Book Ever!

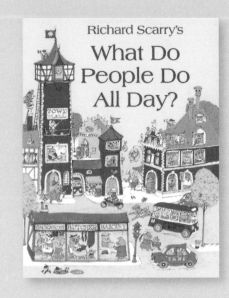

Richard Scarry's What Do People Do All Day?

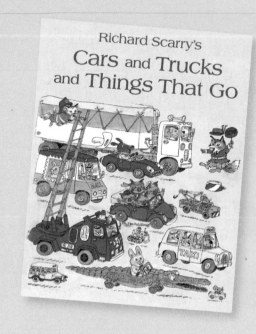

Richard Scarry's Cars and Trucks and Things That Go

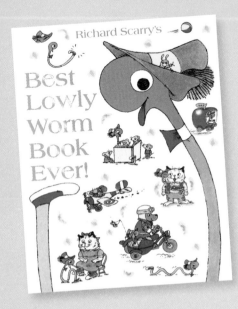

Richard Scarry's Planes and Rockets and Things That Fly

Richard Scarry's A Day at the Airport

Richard Scarry's Best Bedtime Stories Ever